KB268208

서른세 줄기 바람의 시

Poems of Thirty-Three Voices
Carried on the Wind

Translated by Sue LaPlant

서른세 줄기 바람의 시

Poems of Thirty-Three Voices
Carried on the Wind

초판 1쇄 인쇄 | 2010년 1월 25일
초판 1쇄 발행 | 2010년 2월 1일
지은이 | 워싱턴문인회
옮긴이 | Sue LaPlant
펴낸이 | 조종현
펴낸곳 | 북오션

종 이 | 대한실업
출 력 | 푸른서울
인 쇄 | 정민문화
출판신고번호 | 제313-2007-000197호

주 소 | 서울시 마포구 서교동 468-2번지
이메일 | bookrose@naver.com
전 화 | (02)322-6709
팩 스 | (02)3143-3964

ISBN 978-89-93662-13-9 (03800)

워싱턴 문인 시선집

서른세 줄기 바람의 시

Poems of Thirty-Three Voices
Carried on the Wind

Translated by Sue LaPlant

북오션

워싱턴에서 시를 사랑하는 사람들이 한국어를 주로 사용하는 이민 1세대와 영어를 사용하는 2세대 간에 일상적인 대화의 소통을 넘어 가슴속 심연의 마음을 통해 진정 하나의 정서로 묶는 것이 무엇인가를 생각해 왔습니다.

그러다 자연스럽게 1세대가 한국어로 쓴 시를 2세들이 읽고 느낄 수 있는 영시로 번역 출판하자는 공감대가 이루어졌습니다.

서른 세 명의 시인들이 쓴 시를 영역하는 과정에서 서로 만남이나 교분을 나눈 적이 전혀 없는 분들이 일관된 논평을 해주셨습니다.

본국에서 발표되는 한국시도 미국에서 흔히 접하는 미국시도 아닌 독특한 시의 세계를 이루고 있다는 것입니다.

아마도 그것은 워싱턴에 둥지를 튼 우리들만의 시의 세계를 말함일 것입니다.

이제 우리는 이민 2세, 더 나아가 후세들과의 교감을 갖는 것을 넘어 우리들만의 독특한 시의 세계를 연 것을 자랑스럽게 생각하면서 소수 이민자뿐만 아니라 영어권의 여러분들과도 함께 나누고자 합니다.

시를 쓰는 사람들은 시가 주는 위로와 시의 힘을 알고 있습니다.

문학은 독자와의 소통이 있어야 완성 되는 것이므로 그 지평을 넓히는 데 우리도 노력을 함께 할 것입니다.

많은 명상 센터에서 이미 시를 치료의 방법으로 선택하고 있다는 사실에 기뻐하며 힘을 얻습니다.

시를 번역해주신 분들, 미국에서 대학을 마치고 꾸준히 영어와 한국어로 시를 써오던 Sue LaPlant씨와 미국과 한국대학에서 교수직을 역임, 다수의 시집과 영문시집을 출간하신 최연홍 시인, 미국대학에서 영문학을 전공한 최은화님께 감사를 드립니다.

또한 감수를 맡아주신 두분, 미국대학에서 언어학, 독일 대학원에서 비교언어학으로 세계 여러 나라 언어와 문화를 접해온 전(이)인묵씨와 한국어를 전혀 모르지만 동양과 특별한 관계를 가진 후손으로 문학적 분위기에서 자라온 S씨 (이름 밝히기를 사양)께 깊은 감사를 드립니다.

Foreword

Among the members of the poetry−loving literary society here in Washington, DC, there was a strong desire to create an opportunity for the Korean-speaking first generation and the English-speaking second generation to share not only their experiences in everyday life but also their innermost thoughts, emotions and feelings. The general consensus among us was to have our Korean poetry translated into English to achieve that goal.

Unlike most poems that are presented in Korea or in United States, this is a unique project. This collection offer a glimpse of our society, enjoying the comfortable shelter and communion here in Washington, DC area.

With this book, we hope to reach not only the English-speaking second generation, but also future generations here and abroad and let them enjoy and appreciate the manifestations of our pride in the outstanding and distinguished poets among us.

Poets breathe and soak in the comfort and the power that come from poetry. Literature is complete only when the writer and the reader can communicate and become one, and we are steadfast in our determination to achieve such a level of perfection.

We are encouraged and pleased to know that poetry

is being used to treat those that are in need of emotional or mental healing.

Among those who helped with the translation are Sue LaPlant who after completing her higher education in the United States continued to write poetry both in Korea and the United States, poet Yearn Hong Choi who taught at universities in Korea and U.S. and have published many collections of poetry both in Korean and in English, and finally Ms. Eun Wha Choi who had studied English in the USA.

Further gratitude goes to two proofreaders: In Mook (Lee) Chun who studied languages in the USA and continued graduate studies in Germany, and an anonymous helper (who did not want his name disclosed), who grew up among the literary surroundings and though lacking knowledge in Korean language, has special ties with Korea.

 차례

글머리에

1부

2부

3부

1부

이제 단 하나 남은

강혜옥

이제 세상에
이런 류의 주조식 철교는
주황빛 페인트가 덧칠된
이것 하나 남았다고
리틀 파툭센트 강 다리에
작은 놋쇠판이 붙어 있다

일상처럼 건너는
그 다리 위에서는
낡은 풍향기가 높이 걸린
붉은 벽돌 건물이 보인다
그 벽돌 사이로 난 유리창 하나를
소유하고 싶은 나는
해지는 무렵까지
햇빛에 빛나는 그 다리를
노상 보고싶어서이다
그렇게 너도
이제 단 하나 남은 다리이다

내 탯줄이 묻힌 산천을 잇는

The Sole Surviving One

Hae Ock Kang

Translated by Hea Ock Kang

'Bollman Iron Truss Bridge, 1869 Spanning the
Little Patuxent River
Is the sole surviving …'
Is written on a plaque on the persimmon red
bridge

Crossing the bridge daily,
Looking up the rustic brick building
With an old wind pane hanging high on the top
I longed to own one of those windows between
the bricks
Looking down the bridge
To always keep the bridge shining with twilights
in my sights
Until the sun sets

Likewise,
You are the only bridge remaining for me

To connect to the site where my umbilical cord's
memories are buried

숲의 계승 I

이 숲은 30년 전에는 그저 잡초나 자라던 들판이었다
어느 날 새 한 마리가 너도밤나무 씨앗을 떨어뜨리고 갔다
그 한 그루의 너도밤나무는 숲의 계승을 시작했다
이제는 새벽안개가 깊이 휘감아 돌아나오는 너도밤나무
숲이 되었다

The Succession Of the Forest

This forest used to be a mere field covered with
grasses and bushes
Till on a day a bird dropped a beech tree seed

The beech seed then sprouted to start a
succession of a forest
Now, it became a beechwood, laced with
morning mist
Deeply between the trees

고요의 속

권귀순

강물이 바다와 만나는 곳에 갔었다
강물은 언제 우나
오래 지켜 앉아도 울지를 않네

흔적도 없이 제 몸을 주어버리면서
너무 고요하기만 하네

저 고요의 발에는 물갈퀴가 있다고 해야 하나
물위에 유유히 떠 있는 물오리처럼

고요만 떠오르게 하고는
강물 깊은 곳에서는 울고 있다고 해야 하나

수수한 어머니가
어둠 속에서 몰래 울던 것처럼
모든 평온에는
안 보이는 물갈퀴가 있다고 해야 하나

강물 속을 들여다봐도, 귀기울여 봐도
고요의 속은 알 수 없네
갈대밭 쓸고 가는 바람 소리뿐
강물인지 바다인지 경계가 없네

아무 일도 일어나지 않은 듯
고요의 속은 들리지 않네

The Inside Of Silence

Kwi Soon Kwon

Translated by Andy Kim

I was where the river met the ocean
When does the river cry?
Been sitting and watching long, never seen it cry

It gives away everything, leaving out nothing
Still, it keeps silent

Is it fair to say that its silence has web feet?
Like a duck who floats around on the water

Is it fair to say that it lets the silence rise to the

surface
And weeps in the deep of the river?

Like a mother of plain living who weeps secretly
in the dark
Is it fair to say that all quietness has the invisible
web feet?

I look into the inside of the river, I listen to the
sound
Still no way to know the inside of silence

All I hear is the sound of the wind sweeping the
reed field
I see no boundary between river and sea

As if nothing happened
I hear nothing from the inside of silence

그믄 여자

중환자실 문이 열릴 때마다 소스라칠 듯 동그랗게
열리는 그 여자의 창
간절하게 애원하듯 순식간에 열렸다 스르르 닫힌다
누군가를 온몸으로 기다리는 그 여자
사는 일은 기다림이라고 말하던 때 엊그제 같다
구멍 난 흙벽을 바르고 군불을 지피고 담 밑에
봉숭아를 심던 엊그제
방탄유리 속에서 밥을 벌고 아이들 가르치고
방탄유리 벗어날 꿈을 꾸던 엊그제
한 기다림이 다른 기다림에게 서늘한 마디를 넘기던
그 시린 엊그제
폭설을 견디는 나무가 제 가지를 툭, 툭, 부러뜨리며
울던 밤에도 그 여자는 창을 열어 놓았다
나무울음 사이로 눈을 건너오는 발소리 들릴까 하고
이제 창을 닫아 줄 때라는 걸 안다
기다림이 업이던 그 여자 기다릴 시간이 없다는 걸 안다
달이 이울듯이 그 여자는 이울어
기다림을 들여놓은 마음이 쿵, 하고 무너진다
그 여자는, 그 여자는 그믈었다
이너하버 하스피탈 중환자실에서 그 여자의 기다림도
마침내 그믈었다

한 잎의 눈송이처럼 나풀나풀, 나-풀-나-풀

Dimming Woman

Translated by Eunhwa Choe

Her window to the soul opens startlingly, whenever the door to her intensive care unit opens; they opened instantly in ardent appeal and gently and softly closed.

The woman waits, with her whole being, for someone.

It seems like only yesterday when she said, "Living is waiting."

Yesterday, when the hole in the mud-plastered wall was filled, the fire stoked to heat the floors, and Touch-Me-Nots were planted on the base of the wall.
Yesterday, when living was earned and children taught behind the bullet proof glass walls and the dreams of escaping the bullet proof glass wall were dreamt.

Yesterday, on that achingly chilly day, one waiting left cold words to the another waiting.
Even in the icy storm evenings, when the trees wept as the branches broke off, she had her windows open, anticipating the sound of feet trodding through the snow, amidst the sound of trees weeping.

She knows it's now a time to close the window.

She, whose vocation was waiting, knows she no longer has the time to wait.

As the moon wanes, the woman wanes too, as the heart filled with the waiting collapses with a thud.

The woman, the woman dimmed.

The woman's waiting finally dimmed too, in the intensive care unit of the Harbor Hospital Center.

Like a fluttering snowflake, she flutters, flutters, f–l–u–t–t–e–r–s.

부모 마음

권영은

아래로 아래로만 가는 것이
흐르는 물뿐이랴

나의 전부라는 말은 차마 못하지만
네가 없는 나의 모습은
전혀 그릴 수가 없구나

내 살을 베어 주어도
그 상처는 흉터도 없이 이내 아물고
가슴 무너져 내려도
너는 나에게
언제나 다시 피는 꽃이란다

사랑의 결실이며
사랑의 책임
나의 분신이면서도
너는 내가 아니기에
품고만 있을 수 없으니

이만치 떨어져서
말 없이 지켜보고만 있으리라
기다리리라
눈물로 다가와도
웃음으로 뛰어와도
양팔 벌려 너를 맞이하리라

아래로 아래로 흐르는 것이
어디 물뿐이랴

Parents' Affection

Youngeun Kwon
Translated by Sue LaPlant

Water isn't the only thing
that flows from the high to the low

Though I dare not say you are everything to me
I cannot at all imagine
a life without you

Even if my flesh is carved out for you
Its wound heals fast without a scar

Even when you break my heart
You are always a beautiful blossom
Readily born again in my heart
A fruit of love
A duty for love
You are a part of me and yet
You are not I
So when you fly away from the nest
I will still watch over you
Quietly from a nearby place

I will wait
Even if you come to me as tears
Or run to me as a smile
I will greet you with open arms

Water isn't the only thing
That flows from the high to the low

스무 살을 맞는 아들에게

햇살을 먹고
빗물을 마시며
바람의 보살핌에
스무 해 굵어진 뿌리가
제법 자리를 잡는 것 같구나

지난 겨울들은 견딜 만했었기에
길어지는 봄볕 아래
지금부터 꾸는 너의 꿈이
화려하기보다는 아름답기를
나도 꿈꾸어 본다.

이제는 더욱 푸르러지기를
두려운 번개빛
온몸 흔드는 천둥에도
단단한 가지를 키워 내는 여름날을
너는 감사로 노래할 수 있어야 한다.

하늘을 우러르고
땅을 의지하는 겸손함도
작은 들꽃에게 눈길을 보낼 수 있는

넉넉하고 따뜻한 마음까지도
모두 네 안에 있다면 참 좋겠구나.

찾지 않아도 손닿을 만큼 떨어져서
부르면 답할 수 있을 만한 상거에서
언제고 기다리고 있으리라
내 사랑하는 너를

To My Son as You Turn 20

Fed on sunshine
Rainwater as a drink
Well-cared by the winds
Twenty years thus far prepared you
Adequately to stand tall

You endured the past winters well
Now under the longer days of spring sunlight
What you dream hence forth
Shall be beautiful rather than glorious
I, too, dream your dream

Let young heart be filled with fresh dreams
Don't be afraid of fierce lightening

nor the shuddering of roaring thunder
Rather, sing of gratitude for the challenges
that make you stronger

Goals as high as the sky
Humbleness to lean on the earth
Caring attitude to the insignificant matters
Generous and warm heart
I hope they all will live in your heart

I will live within your arm's reach
Close enough to answer your calling
I will always wait for you
My beloved son

산에서 부는 바람

김경암

산새들의 노래는
허공에서 부는 산바람의 시
한 점의 그림은
구도자의 자비를 심어 주는 웃음
한 자의 글귀는
가끔 길 잘못드는 중생들 마음에
이정표를 세워 주는 산바람이네
욕심도 성냄도 벗어놓고
미움도 사랑도 내려놓은 이 마음
강이 되어 바다로 흐르네

Wind from the Mountain

Kyoung Am Kim

Translated by Yearn Hong Choi

The mountain bird's song is the poetry of the
wind
Blowing from the high land to the low land.

One landscape painting is the Buddha's smile,
Showing his Love and Mercy to the masses.

Human language is making a scripture,
Guiding the masses who lost their way in the
wilderness.

Leaving my heavy burden, ambition and anger to
the low land,
My mind is flowing as a river toward the sea, as
the wind.

입학기도

바람의 조바심도 산을 넘는다
보성의 고갯마루
쌀 한 되, 초 한 자루 가슴에 품고
부처 찾아간 긴 한나절

맑은 물은 개울가 바위 틈에 졸고
산비둘기 날아와 구구구구구
목마른 기원을 아는 듯 반겨 주네

마음은 부처님께 바치고
눈과 귀를 법당에 들여놓고
부처의 지혜로 잘 보고 들어라

사랑하는 나의 아들, 딸들
염불로 타들어가는
시공

공연히 부모들이 대리시험
보는구나

Mother's Prayer

*— for her children's successful college entrance
exam —*

Mother's impatience on the mountain trail
And on the hill of the wind
With one toe of rice and one dozen candles
Comes to pray in front of the Buddha's image.

Clean water in the creek
Flowing through the rocks and
Mountain pigeons
coo coo coo coo
Are greeting the mother's thirst.

Her mind is dedicated to Buddha,
Her eyes and ears are parts of the sermon hall.
See and hear the things with His wisdom!

Her love is burning like a candle
With the monk's invocation
In the sacred time and space.

Mother is taking the college entrance test
On behalf of her son and daughter.
Alas! What is she doing?

미끄럼틀

김 령

그때 나는 수백 년 묵은
느티나무 그늘 아래 놓여 있던 미끄럼틀 위에서
미끄러져 내려가고 있었지
한 발짝씩 기어올라 맨 꼭대기에 서서
사위 한 번 둘러보고, 눈 딱 감고
내리받이 위에 걸터앉으면
멈출 수도 그만 둘 수도 없었어
아차 싶어 중간에서 벗어날 생각도 했었지만
나는 세상 끝이 어디쯤일지 몰랐지
그러나 오르고 또 올랐어 단지
아무렇지도 않았었다는 기억 하나로
경험을 내려가기 위하여,
쏜살같이 내려가기 위하여 아이들은
모두 제 엉덩이로 파놓은 구덩이 속으로
내리꽂히고 있었어
미끄럼틀이 회전목마가 아니라는 걸 언제
알았을까 사십 년 후 오늘
그늘 드리워 주던 느티나무 아래

내려가기 위하여 제 등 위 오르고 있을 때
그는 내려가고 있었겠지
깊은 뿌리로
오늘은 더 늙었을 느티나무

추억,

휘파람 분다.

A Slide

Ryoung Kim

Translated by Sue LaPlant

Long ago, I rode down the slide
under the Zelkova tree, hundreds of years old
Gliding down
Step by step, I climbed to the top
looked at the surroundings
once I readied at the top and closed my eyes
it was too late to stop or quit
Halfway down at times I wished to get off it
But did not know where the world ended
and yet, climbed it over and over

My only memory was that I was safe
Sliding down, building experience
The faster the better in children's world
slid and fell on the dirt pile
digging holes with our buttocks
Perhaps after forty years, did I just find out
the slide was not a wooden-horse carousel?
Under the shade by the Zelkova tree
we climbed up the trunk, only to slide down,
Even then the tree was reaching downward
Digging deeper with his roots
The tree must be older today

A memory

I whistle.

꿈은 동그랗다

여보세요, 당신은 잠잘 때 고사리
같이 손 꼭 쥐고 잡니까? 아님
곱게 펴고 잡니까 단풍잎같이
그런데 보세요, 모두 다
동그랗지 않아요 살아 있는 것들은
더러는 새벽, 아니 석양에라도 좋아요
다 동그랗게 뜨고 동그랗게 이울어요
해도 이슬도 달도 꽃들도

쥐었다 다시 펴보는 손금처럼
파뿌리 같은 일상 또 들여다보면
약속도 되지 않은 희망에 언제나
가슴 기대고 있는 우리들의 귀로
손가락 사이 흐르는 시간은, 꽃처럼
피었다 지고 또 피고
보이지 않는 시간을 따라 져 내리는
그리움은 항상 벙어리지만
그러나 동그랗고 또 동그라서
구르다 멈춥니다

달과 해, 손잡고 나를 돌고

그것으로 내 마음 나도 재우며
또 하루 동그란 새벽 열었습니다
빛나는 해, 동그란 해바라기씨
하나씩 가슴에 그려 주며
어머니의 목소리로
아침은 열려옵니다, 날마다

꿈은 언제나 수평이 아닌 것 같아요
수직도 물론 아니고요
집 밖으로 나갔던 시계 한 바퀴 돌고 나면
다시 제자리로 돌아오는걸요
보세요, 가을,
열매들이 왜 저렇게 다 동그란가를

동그란 새소리로 해 동그랗게 깨어나고
동그란 꽃봉오리 속 꽃씨 동그랗게 익어가고
동그란 이슬방울 속 빛 동그랗게 잠자고

Dreams Are Round

Do you clench your hands when you sleep
just like spring fern leaf or
open your hands as if a maple leaf?
But look! All of them are
round, all living things
even at dawn or dusk
All rises round and sets round
Sun, dew, moon, and flowers

Just as we trace the creases on our palms
If we retrace our daily lives
We return home filled with unpromised hope
And our hearts are forever seeking and watching
As time flies without waiting for us
Longing always remains a mute
as it flows with invisible time
But it is round, so it rolls and rolls
and it stops now and then

The moon and the sun dance the circle around
as they bring comfort and peace to my heart
Another day begins with a round dawn
Brilliant sun, a round sunflower seed
one by one sow them in my heart

As mother's voice

dawn comes without fail, day after day

Dream is not always horizontal

neither is it vertical

A clock's hands return to their original spot once circled

Look! Fruits in the autumn

How round they are!

Round birds' singing wakes the round sun

Round seeds ripen within round flowers

Round light sleeps within round dew

불러 주소서

김인기

깊고 어두운 골짜기에서
안타까이 헤매고 있습니다
"돌아오라!"고
큰소리로 나를 불러 주소서

님의 가슴에 가시를 박아 놓고
나의 마음 설레며 찾아온 계곡에서
아!
나는 길 잃은 양이 되었습니다

으슥한 곳에서나 쑥스러이 불러 봅니다
님이시여!
범죄의 희열이 사라진 후에
여름날의 먹구름처럼 몰려오는 후회가 있습니다

내 마음 간악하던 그날을 묻지 마시고
큰 소리로 나를 불러 주소서
"돌아오라!"고

Please Call Me

In Gee Kim

Translated by Sue LaPlant

I am in a deep and dark valley
Sadly, strayed from my path
Please call me loudly
 "Come back to me!"

After sticking a thorn that pierced through your heart
I wandered away in excitement to a valley
Ah!
I am now a sheep who has lost his shepherd.

Though awkward, I am calling for you
From this desolate place
My most precious!
The thrill and excitement of sins are now gone
My remorse is hovering over me as
The darkest cloud before a terrific storm

Please do not ask about my wicked past
Just call me loudly
 "Come back to me!"

비에 젖은 새가 되어

당신은
내가 부르기도 전에
대답하는 님이십니다

당신은
내 가슴에 박혀
뜨겁게 타오르는 불화살.
이 몸을 태워 버리는 불떨기입니다

당신은
장마철에 쏟아지는 장대비

나는
억수로 쏟아지는 당신
사랑의 비에 흥건히 젖어서
날아갈 수 없는 한 마리 새입니다

A Bird Drenched in Rain

You
Answer me
Even before I call for you

You are
A flaming arrow burning with passion
Dwelling deeply in my heart
Burning away my total being

You are
A downpour in rainy season

I am
A bird that could not fly away
Drenched in rain
Of your love

2월

김행자

칼바람과 꽃눈 사이
정월과 삼월 사이
아무도 눈여겨보지 않는
생성으로 가는 길
사이사이 빛나는 은밀한 사랑
있어요

새벽정기
이슬 밟고 내려와
삼단 같은 검은 머리 올려주시더니
겨우내 빗장 걸고 숨죽이고 있어도
흙가슴 가슴이 부풀어올랐어요

얼음꽃 몸풀어
마른 가지 옷 입히는 밤
가슴 열어 보여줄래요
내 안에 숨긴 수천의 씨앗을
들리셔요?

몸 안 실핏줄 따라
쿵쿵 물오르는 소리
언 땅 밀어내는 새순의 숨결

만져 봐요
탯줄 지상에 박고
일순, 깜짝깜짝 놀라게 하는
저 생명의 발길질
귀대어 보셔요

February

Haeng Ja Kim

Translated by Yearn Hong Choi

Between snowstorm and crocus bloom
there is a road to a maiden's cottage
no one sees.
Between January and March
there is a secret love, its heat
breaking through the frozen winter land.

When a new dawn falls on the steps
of morning dew, a young man marries

a young woman.
Although the new bride spent all winter
in solitude
her breasts have swollen.

Like ice flowers on the deadly tree branches,
the coming birth is anticipated, a flowered blanket
spread next to the fireplace.
Can you hear the sound?
Water is flowing through
all the veins of the tree.

Please touch me,
a new baby in my womb
is kicking me, so strong.
Oh, I am thrilled by this sign of life.
Please put your ear to my womb.

목련꽃 나무 아래서

앞마당 모퉁이에
백목련이 때늦게 피워 낸 여린
꽃송이를 보고 있으니
탄성보다는 말간 슬픔이
목젖을 타고 오른다

아무도 눈 길 안주는
중년의 목련이
허공에 검푸른 이불 한 채 두르고
살아온 날의 흔적 하나
까치밥처럼 띄워 놓고
고요한 달빛 속에 뒤돌아
앉아 있네

아, 언제였던가
목련꽃 나무 아래서
귓불 달아올라 가슴 콩닥거리던
흘러간 젊은 날의 봄밤이여
일렁이는 바람 속에
가만가만 앞가슴 풀던
수천 수만의 꽃봉오리, 꿈이었어라

가려줄 나뭇잎 한 장 없어도
아침이면 당당히 옷깃 여미고
순백의 금언 들려 주던
그 고고함 다 버리고
서걱이는 잎새들 일제히 흔들어
세월의 강 우르르 건너고 있다

Under the Magnolia Tree

Translated by Eunhwa Choe

At the corner of front yard
Through the exuberant green foliage,
when looking upon a delicate blossom,
bloomed in late season by a white magnolia tree
rather than a sigh, a sheer sadness
rises up through the throat.
 No one looks upon
the middle aged magnolia tree,
with only a dark green coverlet in the air,
a marking of past life,
spread like Spanish needles,
amidst calm moonlight,
it sits turned around.

Ah, when was it.
Under the magnolia tree,
with burning earlobes and throbbing heart,
the past spring nights,
in the undulating wind,
hesitantly opened the breasts,
tens of thousands of blooming buds, those were
the dreams.

Even without a single green leaf for a cover,
in the morning, dressed with confidence,
the golden words of pure white were told.
The proud loneliness tossed aside,
shaking all the crisp leaves,
skipping across the river of time.

아미쉬* 마을

노세웅

화살같이 빠르게 변하는 세상에서
나침판도 없이
어디로 가고 있는가
마차를 타고 워낭소리 딸랑딸랑 울리며 가는
아미쉬 가족

세상 사람들은 낙오자가 될세라
바람처럼 달려가는데
아미쉬 사람들은 유유자적
아직도 16세기에 살고있다.

아스라이 살가운 그 들의 생활철학
아름다이 낭만적인 영농 방식
1950년대 문경새재 고향의 산촌마을 같아

70~80년대에 고향 사람들
젊은 사람들은 서울로 떠났으나
랭케스터, 아미쉬 마을 사람들은

옛날에서 새로움을 찾고
가진 것에 행복해하는 사람들
그래,
새 컴퓨터가 행복을 가져다 줄 수 없고
새 자동차도 행복을 가져다 줄 수 없지
새 집도 행복을 가져다 줄 수 없으나
행복은 자손 대대로 여기 살고 있구나!
나, 여기
행복을 찾으러 왔다.
잃어버린 그 행복을 !

*아미쉬: 네덜란드 사람들 Menno파의 한 분파, Pennsylvania에 이주하여 검소하
게 살고 있음.

The Amish Village

Se Woong Ro

Translated by Yearn Hong Choi

Time is flying like an arrow. I am trying to adjust
myself to the changing times.
Everyone wants not to be far behind the changing
time,
Except for the Amish village people.
They love to preserve their lifestyle in the 16th

century.
I love their philosophy and belief
Their family-centered, labor intensive,
Primitive farming methods with horse power.
Their village is like my Moonkyung mountain
village in the 1950s,
But all my neighbors left for Seoul in the 1970s
and the 1980s.
The Amish people in Lancaster, Pennsylvania are
not looking for changes,
But they are looking for tradition and innovation.
They are happy with what they have.
Yes, new computers cannot bring happiness.
New cars cannot bring happiness.
New houses cannot bring happiness.
Happiness dwells on their old life-style they
cherish.
I myself come to see the happiness in my
childhood days
in the mountain village in Korea.

독도는 외롭지 않아

독도는 한반도에서 머나먼
동해의 외로운 섬, 그러나
독도는 외롭지 않아
동도와 서도가 마주 보고 사랑하고 있잖아
오페라의 연인들처럼

한국인들의 사랑을 받고 있는 독도
미국 미네소타의 선생님과
버지니아의 학생들도
너를 지켜 주고 사랑하고 있어

풍랑이 험한 바다에서
파선된 어부들의 생명을 지켜 주는
의(義)로운 섬 이지
외로운 섬이 아니야

독도는 고독한 섬, 그래서
한국인들과 세계인들이
지켜 주고 사랑하고 싶은 섬

역사(歷史)책을 읽어봐

삼국사기, 삼국유사, 고려사, 그리고
이조실록과 고지도(古地圖)에도
독도는 우리 땅

일본인들이여
도둑질하려 하지 마라
독도를 사랑하는 사람들에게서
외로운 섬, 독도를.

Lonesome Island, Dokdo

Dokdo is a lonesome island in the East Sea
far from the Korean Peninsula.
But it is not sorrowful.
Dokdo is two islets,
the East and the West Islands
like the two lovers in an opera.

Dokdo has been loved by the Korean people
plus one American school teacher in the
Minnesota,
and many students in the Virginia
because it is a lonesome island
in the stormy sea,

but it is a nice shelter for the fishermen who lost
their boat in the stormy sea.

Dokdo is a lonesome island,
So it has been loved by all Korean people and
foreign people.

Please explore the Korean history books,
Samkook Sagi, Samkuk Yusa, Koryo Sa, and Yijo
Silrok, and old maps.

Japanese people, never attempt to steal the
Dokdo
from those who love the lonesome island.

저녁미사

박 앤

사제의 행렬을 비추며
채색유리를 통해 들어온 해거름의 붉은 햇빛
저녁 미사가
오늘은 분심 속으로 나를 밀어 넣었다
그치지 않고 뒤에서 들리는 소곤대는 소리

흘낏 뒤돌아보자
민망한 듯 눈길을 피하는 할아버지와
지그시 눈을 감고 쓰러질 듯 기대앉은 할머니
들릴 듯 말 듯 웅얼거리는 여전한 소리

미사가 끝난 후
할아버지의 부축을 받으며
더듬더듬 걸어나가는 할머니 손에 쥐어진 하얀 지팡이
눈 먼 할머니에게 예절이 진행되는 것을
할아버지는 귓속말로 일러주고 있었구나

마지막 석양이

노부부의 등에 잠시 머물다가 사라졌다

– 주님, 자비를 베푸소서 –

불현듯 미사 경문의 한 구절
뭉클해진 내 가슴속을 뚫고 나와
텅 빈 성당 안을 울리다가 사라졌다

Evening Mass

Anne Park

Translated by Eunhwa Choe

Lighting the priest's procession,
Through the stained glass, was the crimson dusk
sunlight.
At this evening Mass,
I am moved to distraction
By constant whispers coming from the back.

When I glance back,
There is an old man avoiding eye contact in
embarrassment
And an old woman leaning toward him with

closed eyes.
The sound of murmuring continues.

After the mass,
I see the old woman supported by the old man,
As the old woman gropes her way with a white
cane
The old man had been explaining the progress of
the mass
To the blind old woman

The last of the dusk sunlight
Lingered on the couple's back before fading
away.

– Christ Have Mercy on Us –

Suddenly this phrase from the Mass
Pierced my constricted heart
And rang through the empty chapel before fading
away.

못 다 지은 집

지푸라기 몇 올, 나뭇가지 몇 개
걸쳐놓았을 뿐

차고 서까래에
집을 짓던 새 한 쌍
어느 날 큰 소리로 토닥거리다
홀연히 버리고 떠났네
못 다 지은 집

알을 까고 새끼를 품어
일가의 보금자리 될
우주의 중심
그 집에 바람만 들다 간다

버려진 집은
쓸쓸하고 적막해
언제쯤 느껴볼 것인가
들었던 주인의 체온 한 줌

A House Not Finished

Just a handful of straws, a couple of sprigs
Did they put into place

On the sloping beams of the garage
A bird couple was building a house
One day I heard loud wrangling
Gone are they in a flash into the thin air
Leaving behind a house not finished

Laying eggs, brooding
They could have made a nest home for the family
The center of the universe
Now it's only wind that comes and goes

The abandoned house is
Lonely and forlorn
When can I feel the warmth?
The warm temperature of the house owners that
left

아버지의 상흔

박양자

이른 새벽 잠 깨우는 이름 모를 새 소리 밖엔 추적추적
비가 내리고 나는 까치발로 나가 빗방울 맺힌 비닐 봉투
에서 신문을 꺼내들고 세상을 읽는다 광복 60주년! 순간
가슴이 뭉클하다

아버지의 벗은 몸엔 동그란 무늬가 여러 개 있었다 어릴
적 손가락으로 짚으며 숫자 셈을 하던 판화 같던 무늬 그
내력을 안 것은 초등학교 입학 후였다 열일곱 나이에 밤
새 등사판으로 인쇄한 수천 매의 격문을 돌리고 '총독부
폭압 정치 절대 반대' '피압박 민족 해방 만세' 의 깃발을
제작하여 거리에 나섰던 학생들의 투혼, 그 옥고 치를 때
당한 흔적임을 어렴풋이 알게 되었다 가끔 독립만세의
아우성과 호각 소리에 쫓기듯 자다가 벌떡 일어나 한참
씩 댓돌 위에 서 계셨던 아버지, 그 후유증의 고통을 광
복의 기쁨으로 묵묵히 견디셨으리

고향에 돌아가 한라산 기슭 아흔아홉 골 선영 솔밭에 누
워 계신 지 이십 년, 입구에 세워진 애국지사 독립 항쟁

기 표지판엔 솔가지 사이로 푸르게 내려 스미는 여름 달
빛 당신 몸 무늬 고스란히 땅 속 흙에 새겨 놓고 온갖 산
새 깃든 나무와 들꽃 가득 피워 조국 번영 기원 축제 한
마당 크게 열었으리 이국에서 맞는 광복절 아침 조간신
문 펼쳐든 내 안에서도 아버지의 상흔이 일어나 서서히
깃발로 펄럭인다

Father's Scar

Yang Ja Park

Translated by Eunhwa Choe

The song of a nameless bird wakes me up early in
the morning, and the rain drizzled outside as I
skipped towards a Korean daily newspaper
protected by plastic covered with rain droplets and
opened the front page, seeing the headline of "60th
Anniversary of Liberation!" My heart constricted
momentarily.

My father had several circles of scars on his body,
and, as a child, I used to feel the imprints of those
circles as if doing sums. It wasn't until I was in
school that I learned the story behind those marks.
When father was seventeen years old, he spent

days and nights copying thousands of petitions and appeals with mimeograph−produced flags. "Against the Oppressive Government General" and "Liberation to Oppressed People" were flags held by students who rallied out in the street, later served time in prison, and received the scars. Father often stood on the stone steps during the nights, awakened from nightmares of being on the run amongst the rallies of liberation chanters and the piercing sound of whistles. He silently withstood the residual sufferings by the joy of the Liberation Day.

It has been years since my father went back to his hometown to lie under the pine needle−covered ancestral grave in the ninety−ninth valley of Mount Halla. On a sign board mounted by the entrance with "Patriotic Fighters of Liberation", the blue of the summer moonlight shimmers through the pine branches to imprint his body on the earth. He is beneath the ground surface as the trees and wild flowers filled with mountain birds had a grand celebration for the 60th anniversary with festivities and wishes of prosperity to our motherland. With the opening of the morning paper in this foreign land, I could feel my father's scars fluttering like flags in my heart.

종유석

수억 년 어둠에 길든 눈빛이
자꾸만 흔들리고 있다
오래 기다려야만
조금씩 다가가는 은밀한 수고가
얼마나 더 길어야 머리 맞댈 수 있을지
얼마나 더 깊어야 손 깍지 낄 수 있을지
허공에 긴 손가락 내밀고
마음으로 셈하는
숨소리 같은 초침 소리
하루, 열흘, 천 날, 만 날,
눈물 없이는 가까이 갈 수 없어
오로지 손끝으로
끊임없이 울어야 하는데
말간 손풍금 소리 같은 울음
똑…… 또로록,
석순 정수리에
눈물 떨어지는 소리
언 동굴 속 깊숙이 둥지 틀고 있다

Stalactite

An eye deeply sitting in darkness
For several hundred million years
Frequently blurring
Long waiting only make an effort
Get close in secret little be little
How much longer to bring heads together
How much deeper to knot fingers together
Stretch a long finger in the air
Counting in mind
A sound of second hand like breathing
One day, ten days, thousand days, ten thousand
days
Can not go near without tears
Only fingertip
Must be crying like a clear hand−organ
Drip······ drip,
The crown of the head of stalagmite
The sound of tear−drop
It builds a nest in a deep freezing cave.

깊은 숨에 잠기다
– 라인하트의 그림 'Black' 을 보며 –

박현숙

아무 말도 하지 않았다, 다만
본연의 색
해와 달이 없는 우주가 들어가고
캄캄한 자궁
보드랍고 아늑한 물결이 충만하였다.

침묵의 화랑
검은 사각 캔버스
태초의 하늘이었고
물이었다

수천 번의 붓질에
슬픔은 그의 손끝에서 빠져나가고
천 겹의 겨울이 들어서고
잠든 바람을 깨운 후에야
혼돈의 질서가 이루어졌다.

풍피두에서 검은 빛이

심장에 꽂히다

깊은 숨에 잠기다.

*Ad Reinhardt: 미국태생의 추상 화가이며 파리 풍피두 센터에 그의 그림이 걸려
있다.

Submerged in Deep Thoughts
– Viewing the painting, 'Black' by Ad Reinhardt –

Hyun Sook Park

Translated by Sue LaPlant

No word is spoken, only
The true color
The universe existed without the sun and moon
A dark womb
Was filled with soft and comfortable waves

A silent art gallery
On a black rectangular canvas hanging on the wall
It was the beginning of the sky
and water

Through the thousands of strokes
Sorrows flew out of his fingertips
A thousand winters stepped in one after the other
Only after awakening the sleeping winds
The chaos was calmed to order

In the hall of Pompidou,
Black light pierced into the heart

Submerged in deep thoughts

아버지

퇴근하고 돌아오신 아버지
마루에 걸터앉아
물 가득 담은 놋대야에 발을 담그신다
시원해진 발만큼 훤해지던 아버지의 젊은 모습
온종일 삶을 지탱하고 있던 발 내려놓으며
담 너머 어둑해오는 골목길 망연히 보시던 아버지

불혹의 나이 들어선 안개 속 나날
앞마당 무화과 막 열리던 초여름
무엇을 생각하셨을까
아득한 꿈 하나 세우며
먼 바다 향한 마음 키우고 계셨을까

문을 열고 들어서는
아직도 한결같이 고요한 저 노인
내 아버지 발을 씻겨 드리고 싶다
태평양 건너, 참으로 먼 길 온 겸손한 발
그 앞에 무릎꿇고
움츠린 발가락 천천히 풀어 드리고 싶다

Father

Coming home after a day of work
Father sits at the edge of the wooden floor
Soaks his feet in the copper basin filled with water
to the brim
The look of relief brightens father's youthful face
Resting down the feet that carried
All the toils of the day
He stared out in a daze into the dimming street

The foggy days when he turned forty
The early summer that invited the fruit of figs
What was he thinking?
Was he building a dream in his heart
And yearning for the far- away ocean?

The door opens and
In walks the still serene old man
I long to wash the feet of my father
The feet that crossed the ocean on a long journey
But still modest
I wish to kneel down before them
And slowly straighten the toes one by one
That are shrunk and curled up

2부

자주 댕기

오요한

이름 하나 있어
가슴 속

잊을 듯
잊은 듯, 잊혀지지 않는
얼굴 하나
밤마다
호롱불로 타오릅니다.

종착역이 어디란 걸 알고는 있지만
무진같이 누벼온 세월
정작 삶은 지금도 미로입니다.

길 가다, 가다
우연히,
정말 우연히라도
보고 싶은 이름 그 얼굴
사십 년 지난 오늘에도

머무르지 않는 바람
그리움인가
그 소녀
자주빛 댕기

A Purple Hair Ribbon

John Oh
Translated by Sue LaPlant

The Only name
Deep in my heart

As if forgotten
Perhaps forgotten, and yet, no, cannot be forgotten
The one face
Every night
Dances like the flame of kerosene lamp

Though the final destination is known
Lived the life as if there is no end
Yet even now, life is full of mystery

As we walk on and on the road

By a truly accidental encounter
Yes, even if just by chance
The face we long to see, the name we wish to call
Even today after 40 years
The wind does not linger

Must be the yearning
The young girl
With her purple hair ribbon

황톳길

잊을 수가 없었네
세월 따라 흘러온 어제
가시밭 헤치며 지나온 기억
코뚜레 낀 황소 달구지
보리섬 싣고 가던 길

지울 수가 없었네
까치집 매달린 버드나무
덕하 장터 십 리 길 돌아
고무신 연필 박하사탕
신문지에 꼭꼭 싼 어머니 종종걸음

버릴 수 없었네
실내천 잘 자란 보리
노란 리본 맨 계집아이 웃음
황토도 시간도 다 묻어버린 기억
노을에 걸린 내 고향 황톳길

A Yellow Clay Road

I could not forget
Yesterday brought by time
A memory of weaving through the thorn bush field
An ox with a nose ring, pulling a cart of barley sacks

I could not erase
A weeping willow with a bird's nest
Mother's hurried steps, carrying rubber shoes,
Pencils, peppermint candies wrapped in newspapers
From the Dukha market miles away

I could not part from
Tall barley growing near a small brook
The laughter of a girl wearing a yellow ribbon
Buried memories of yellow clay and time
A yellow clay road of my hometown under the glowing sky

개나리

유경찬

봄이 얼마나 너를 사랑했길래
그 많은 꽃들을 제쳐놓고서
개나리 너를 앞세웠구나

아마도 노오란 꽃잎이 보고 싶어
산들바람 봄바람을 불러서
아름다운 너를 오도록 했겠지

그 순간에 넌 그렇게도 좋아서
파아란 잎새의 친구도 제쳐놓고
샛노란 꽃부터 피웠으니 어쩌면 좋아!

허지만 봄과 함께 피어온 너의 모습에
온 누리에 기쁨이 넘쳐흐르니
너는 정말로 개나리 개나리 꽃이로구나

흙 모래 뒤집어 쓰고 사막을 질러
먼 길 타향에 고향길 오는 길섶에서
젊은 날의 그들에게 꽃피워 반겨준 넌데

Forsythia

Kyung Chan Yoo

Translated by Sue LaPlant

How deeply must spring have loved you
Out of all flowers
He picked you to lead

Perhaps he missed your yellow petals
He must have charmed the soft breeze of spring
To bring forth beautiful you

Unable to restrain your excitement of anticipation
You came rushing, forgetting your green−leaf friends
Only to bloom in yellow flowers!

The entire universe is overjoyed
At the appearance of you in spring
You are forsythia, indeed the flower among flowers!

Across the desert of dirt and soil
I came to this unfamiliar land after a long journey
Along the roadside, you greeted me in my youth
with a beautiful smile

나 아니면

그렇게
보고 싶고 그립고 그리워서
가슴 조아리며 기다리는 마음을
나 아니면 아무도 모르리

그리고
생각만으로 지면을 채우려는 순간들도
그리운 마음으로 사랑이 가득한 것을
나 아니면 아무도 모르리

저
강물 흐르듯 인생도 흘러버린
세월속의 허전한 틈새로 기다려 보는 심사는
나 아니면 아무도 모르리

어느 땐
보름달 뜨고 별들이 총총히 어울린 밤이 오면
별들의 속삭임이 얼마나 부러웠는가를
나 아니면 아무도 모르리

If Not I

Such
Missing and longing and more longing
Heart of waiting cannot be contained
If Not I, no one would know

And then
Though I desperately attempted to write only the
thoughts
They are flooded with deep longing and love
If not I, no one would know

Like a river
Life has flown away
With every passing moment
The empty heart still waits with hope
If not I, no one would know

On some nights
With the full moon and the million stars together
How I envied their sweet whispering in the sky
If not I, no one would know

먼 그대

유양희

지금쯤 그 사람도
가을이 되었을까

잎새마다
프리즘을 스치다 멈춰 버린
빛들의 아름다운 슬픔

눈 먼 바람
마른 잎 흔드는 소리
세월이 지는 소리

먼 풍경도
서로 만나 인사하는
가을날 오후

가까이 있어도
만날 수 없어
더욱 그리운 그 사람

Faraway You

Yang Hui Yu

Translated by Sue LaPlant

I wonder, by now
if he, too, has become an autumn

In the midst of building our rainbow
with purity and luminous colors
abruptly dissipated, sad beauty of a story

Blind winds
sound of dried leaves rustling
silence of time elapsing

Landscapes even in the far distance
meet and greet each other
in this afternoon of an autumn

We live nearby and yet
Too far for a reunion
Intensifying my yearning even more

안개

하늘이 쓸쓸해
지상으로 무너진 구름인가
안개는 어쩌자고
내 앞을 가로막는가

세상의 길을 지우고
마음도 흐려 놓고
오늘은 한 번쯤
가지 않은 길을 가보라 하네

현실에 저당 잡힌 시간들이
비로소 내게 돌아와
흰 슬픔으로
나를 위로하는 아침

살아갈수록
살아가는 일이 더욱 낯설어
대책 없이 목메는데

저만치서 안개 속에
신호등이 파랗게 웃고 있네

Fog

Have the clouds tumbled down
Because the sky was too lonely
Why does the fog
Obscure my view

Erased the paved roads
Cause an opaqueness to my mind
And tells me to explore a new route
One I never traveled before

Time borrowed from the present
Is finally returned to me
As white sorrows
Comfort me this morning

The longer I live
The more foreign the daily life
Makes me fumble without a solid plan

At a near distance
A green traffic light smiles at me

뼈의 노래

윤미희

구십 평생을 말 없이 지켜 온
아버지의 굽은 등을 눕혔을 때
시간의 태엽이 풀리고 있었다

아버지의 시간은 유효기간이 지난 듯
또 다시 꽃이 되어 피질 못했다
시간의 전원이 꺼지자
그의 내부가 순식간에 어두워졌다
살아 의미가 되었던 수많은 꽃잎들이
형체를 잃고 분열했다
가장 먼저
나에게 꿈을 수혈 해 준 심장의 꽃물이
눈물처럼 흐르고 있었다
한잎……
두잎……
우울한 저음의 노래가 흐르는 쪽을 향해
소리없이 지워지고 있었다
나는 보았다

꽃잎이 질 때마다
아버지는 알 수 없는 필체로
참회의 시를 쓰고 계셨다는 것을
더 많이 사랑하지 못해 미안했노라고
더 많이 사랑하지 못해 미안했노라고

꽃잎 모두 흩어진 후
마지막 남은 앙상한 꽃대
바람이
허무의 부러진 뼈를 어루만지며
오랫동안 머물러 있었다
시간의 행방을 묻지 않은 채

A Song Born out of Bones

Mi Hee Yoon

Translated by Sue LaPlant

The weary bones of father's back bent
Witnessed the life of 90 years in silence
And the clock continued to wind down
As if to ascertain the passing of fruitful time
He no longer could blossom as a flower again

When the time ran out
There was nothing but empty darkness in him
All those petals that had shed meanings when alive
Have now lost their luster and withered
The essence of a flower from his heart
Had allowed my dreams to blossom
But it is now dripping down like tear drops
One petal······
Two petals······
Toward the droning sound of sad and mournful song
They are being erased soundlessly

I saw
As each petal fell
Father wrote in his illegible style
The poems of regrets and sorrow
Apologizing for not having loved more
Apologizing for not having loved more

When all the petals scattered
Only the thin stem remained
The winds
Caressing the broken bones, no longer fruitful,
Stayed there for a long while
Not asking for the direction of time

밥과 치즈가 섞인다

열네 살 된 큰아이의 밥상 위에
밥과 치즈가 섞인다

그만의 특별메뉴인
뜨거운 밥 위에 치즈를 얹고
소리 없이 두 문화를 섞고 있다

한민족의 뿌리로
미국의 시민으로
힘겹게 가꾸어야 할 이 땅

가끔씩 확인하고 싶은 날은
뜨거운 밥 위에 치즈를 섞으며
두 개의 깃발을 꽂는다
그만의 영토를 가꾼다

Rice and Cheese Mixed

A fourteen year old child's dinner
A mixture of rice and cheese

His own special dish
Added cheese on hot rice
Without a fuss, he is mixing the two cultures

Born as a Korean
Living as an American citizen
Much toil will be required to cultivate this land

When he needs an occasional reaffirmation
He adds cheese to the hot rice
Plants the two national flags
Cultivates his own unique land

노년의 가을

윤학재

고향 땅 흙으로 빚어진 몸이
30년 이민살이로 저녁노을이 되었습니다
물레방아 추억은 아롱아롱 아지랑이 되었고
땀 흘린 타향이 고향 되었습니다

낮을 밤으로 새벽으로 이어오면서
외로워도 그리워도 눈물은 사치스러워
힘들고 몸 아파도 눕지 못하고
땅만 보고 걸어 온 개척자의 길

이제, 숨 고르고 70년 인생길 뒤돌아봅니다
가깝던 사람들 이렇게 저렇게 멀어지고
손에 가진 것, 있어도 그만 없어도 그만
주름진 얼굴만 껍데기로 남았습니다

지난날, 좋았던 것 미웠던 것 다 잊어버리고
걸어온 발자국이 부끄러울 뿐
그저 오늘이 있어 행복하고

손자손녀 품어 보는 것이 보람입니다
낙엽 길을 걸으며
그림자 길게 드리우는 노년의 부부는
거칠어진 죽데기 손 마주잡고
하늘나라 같이 가는 소망이 기도랍니다.

Autumn of a Man

Hark Jae Yun

Translated by Sue LaPlant

Formed from hometown soil
Now I am a man near the sunset
Having lived 30 years as an immigrant
Memories of watermills are only a vague memory
The foreign land where I have toiled is now my
home

Working days and nights
Loneliness and longing persisted
But tears were only for the privileged
Though I suffered from sickness and weariness,
no time to rest was a life

Now having time to breathe, I look back the past
70 years
Those who were once dear to me, now too far away
Whether I possess wealth or not, it matters not
All I am, a wrinkled face, an empty shell
Forgetting love and hate
I am only ashamed, my footprints of the past
I enjoy a small happiness in today's existence
And rewards of long hugs from my grandchildren

Treading on the roads of autumn leaves
Cast long shadows, an old couple hand in hand
We hope and pray for our arrival in heaven together

독도는 우리 아들

반만년 역사로 이 땅을 이어 오면서
오랜 세월 잊어버렸던 내 자식
동해 바다 가운데 외로웠던 너 독도야!

거센 파도 안개 속에 버려졌던 자식
있는지 없는지 모르게 홀대한 너를
이제사 내 자식이라고 부끄럽게 소리치는구나

바다 건너 키 작은 해적들이 너를 앗아가려면
당당한 모습으로 스스로를 지켜온 돌섬아
나는 대한의 자식이라고 용감하게 소리치던 너

바다에서 솟는 해가 너를 보호했구나
파도가 지켜주고 갈매기가 전우였구나
우산도야 다시는 외로워하지 마라

내 피붙이로 태어난 자식
긴 세월 홀로 흘린 외로운 눈물
못난 어미가 이렇게 가슴으로 씻어 주리라
이제는 부모 형제가 너를 떠나지 않으리라
이제는 우리 가슴에 영원히 품으리라

독도는 내 자식 대한민국의 땅이어라!

Dokdo is Our Son

During this land' s history, five thousand years
We have forgotten of you
Standing alone in the midst of East Sea
How lonely must you have been, our son, Dokdo!

A child, abandoned amongst roaring waves and
fogs
We neglected even to check your existence
We now shamefully call you, our son

When short pirates try to steal you away
You, a rock island, protected yourself courageously
Shouting you were a son of Korea

Must have been cared for by the rising sun over the
horizon
Guarded by the waves, seagulls as your comrades
An infinite island, don' t feel lonely any more!

Born as a son inheriting my blood
You have shed lonely tears for a very long time

Now, a shameful mother shall wash away your sorrow

Your parents and siblings will no longer desert you
We will eternally embrace you in our hearts
You are our child, the land of Korea!

바위

이경주

침묵으로 키를 키우는
어느 높이쯤에
바위는 천고로 서 있다

산이 산을 안아 기르듯
침묵과 침묵이 보듬고 포옹하는
피가 들지 않는 가슴

어느 날
말문 열리는 날 있어
피가 도는 목숨으로 다시
일어설 수 있을까?

바위는
영원한 생명의 입상으로
숨쉴 수 있는 그 날을
오늘도 침묵으로 기다린다

A Rock

Kyung Joo Lee

Translated by Sue LaPlant

Raised by eternal silence
it grew to a proper height
A rock stands as it endured a billion years

As the mountain raises a mountain within his bosom
the silence embraced and nurtured
and yet no blood flows through its heart

One day
If the communication gate opens
can it wake up as a living thing
with fresh blood circulating?

A rock
waits silently for the day
to be awakened by a breath of life
but for now, it stands as a silent statue

봄은 사시(斜視)다

봄은 사시다
가지들의 곁눈질이 한창이다

바람의 장난기도 심하다
옆구리를 찔러놓고도 시침떼기다
등굽은 나무들의 기지개
가려움을 긁어 떨어뜨리고 살 비늘이
꽃잎으로 쌓여 있다

겨우내 갈라졌던
새 울음에도 윤기가 묻어난다
울음이 노래가 된 때문이리라

생명 있는 모든 것들의 부활
그 축복 아래
저마다의 밀어를 가슴으로 꽃피우며
우리 또한 그렇게
꽃나무로 서 있다

Spring is Strabismus

Spring is strabismus
Tree branches stare sideways

Wild playfulness of the wind
Pokes branches and then pretends as if nothing
Bent trees stretch themselves
And scratch themselves into
Floral petals of flesh scales.

The birds absent during the long gloomy winter
Come back and sing gloriously
Oh, cries must have turned into songs

Resurrection of all living things
Under the blessing of heavens
Each blossoming from its secret place
Just like flowers from the heart
We, too, stand there
As flowering trees

네잎 클로버

이영자

나뭇가지 사이로 햇살내리고
신선한 바람을 타고
새들은 속삭여요.

이슬에 젖은 풀냄새
품어 안고 있으니
마음에 간직한 꿈 이야기가
듣고 싶어지는군요.

그렇게 머뭇거리지만 말고
숲 향기 스미는 여기서
우리 마음을 열면
좋은 일이 있을 것 같네요.

내 이름은 작고
연약한 들풀이지만
행운의 기쁨 안겨 드리는
네잎 클로버예요.

여기저기
어디에서도
열려 있는 내 마음이에요

Four-leaf clover

Young Ja Lee

Tanslated by Yearn Hong Choi

The sunshine is coming down through the
branches.
The birds are chirping in the cool wind.
Grass with fresh morning dew wants to listen
To your dream last night which is still vivid in
your heart.
Don't hesitate, my dear.
Plesae tell me your dream within this fragrance of
the woods.
Once you open your heart, all good things will
happen.
My name is a small and vulnerable wild grass,
But I can offer you a fortune.
Here and there, wherever,
My heart is open.

사람이 죽으면 온 곳으로

자연을 대하였을 때
우리 마음이 좋은 것은

사람이 흙으로 만들어졌기
때문인가 보다

앉아 있을 때보다
누웠을 때가 더 편안한 것은

사람이 흙과 가까워졌기
때문인가 보다

사람의 호흡이 끊어지면
몸은 흙으로 돌아가고

영은 하나님께로부터 와서
다시 하늘나라 본향으로 되돌아가니

사람이 죽으면 온 곳이 있기에
돌아갔다고 하는가 보다
때가 되면 언제고 떠나야 하는

사람은 누구나 시한부 인생

그래서 장차 돌아갈 하늘나라가
나의 소망이 되는가 보다

Returning to the Original Place

I feel good when I face the nature.
Do you know why?
Because I am made of earth.

I feel more comfortable when I lie down.
Than I sit down.
Do you know why?
Because I am closer to earth when I lie down.

After my last and final breath,
My body will return to earth,
And my spirit goes back to the homeland,
The original place
Where I came from.

When we pass away,
We all return to the original place
Where we came from.

We all die when time comes,

So the homeland becomes our hope and aspiration.

치매 노인 병동

이은애

시골 부뚜막 위
말라붙은 삼베 보자기
주름살 가득 찬 얼굴에
백치의 웃음이 흐른다

먼 공간을 방황하는 눈빛
무엇에 쫓기는 초조가 가득하고
다가오는 손길이 너무 간절해
그리움의 물이 고인다

생존욕마저
오랜 망각 속에 흩어지고
어린아이 밥투정은
오히려 아름답다

열심히 쌓아온 생활의 방편
어둠 속에 찾을 길 없고
웃음을 전하는 원초적 감각은

새로운 길을 틔운다

불기는 사라지고
붉은 형상이 사그라진 삼나무 재
끈질긴 삼베 줄기의 모진 생명
잊혀 가는 사랑의 그림이
노인 병동에 걸려 있다

Old Woman In An Alzheimer Ward

Translated by Eun Ae Lee

On a small country home hearth
Hangs a hemp cloth drying
On a face riddled with wrinkles
Floats a smile of innocence

Her eyes roam and gaze at distant places
As if chased by haunting memories
Yearning for the hands that lie just out of reach
Her eyes well up with teas of longing

Even the last glimmer of zest for life
Has long faded with distant memory

A child' s tantrum at the dinner table
Still brims with desire and life

The memories and experiences of a lifetime
Lie but still and silent in the darkness
The innate impulse to smile
Revives itself in a new host

The spark of fire is now long gone
The embers of the hemp are but ashes
The life of the ever resilient hemp fiber
A fast fading picture of love
Hanging on the wall of the hospital ward
Of an old Alzheimer patient

자화상

먼 산을 바라보며
태우지 못한 불꽃을
머금은 채
그대를 그린다.

빽빽한 숲 속에서
자유로이 뛰놀던 열정은
시간과 함께 가려지고

망각의 침묵 안에
탈바꿈한 모습만이
새롭게 남아 있다

Self Portrait

Looking over mountains afar
And keeping fire vurning in my heart
I have hidden my longing for you

My passion runs freely
In a thick forest of Appalachian Mountains
It fades away into space
Through fleeting time

Yet amidst a sea of forgetfulness
Only my self portrait of born again spirit

Remains like new forever

영어가 나를 웃기네요

이정자

"와이즈맨" 미식 축구공같이 생긴 몸매
텁수룩한 수염에는 치즈부스러기 몇 점 달고
싱글벙글 웃고 다니는 마음씨 착한 흑인
그는 내 가게에 오는 단골손님

한 아름 빨래감 안고 가게 안에 들어서기 바쁘게
누에고치에서 명주실 뽑아내듯
얘기 보따리 풀어 놓는다
귀 활짝 열고 눈은 그의 표정을 쫓아다니며
으흐 으흐 아는 척하며
눈치껏 배꼽을 잡는 시늉도 하며
덩달아 폭소를 터뜨리기도 하지만
나는 내 모습이 웃겨 속에선 눈물 나는데
제 얘기에 취해 흥이 난 그는 엄청 신이 난다

굳은 땅 한 뼘 적시지 못하고
지나가는 한 줄기 소나기처럼
도무지 종잡을 수 없는 그네들의 조크

늦깎이 이민생활 눈치만 웃자라
어눌한 몸짓으로 연출하는 언어,

용수철 튀듯
이글거리는 용광로 속 불덩이 헤치고 솟아오른
노란 민들레
단 한 치의 척박한 땅에도 뿌리박는
질긴 속성, 은근한 꽃잎
동녘 하늘가에 실안개처럼 피어나는
모국어로 건져 올린 시 한 줄 읊으면
오! 감미로운 이 속살의 떨림이여

English Makes Me Laugh

Chong Cha Lee

Translated by Eunhwa Choe

His body is shaped like a wiseman football
A few crumbs of cheese cling on his bristly beard
The good-natured, the smiling black man
Is a regular customer at cleaners

When he walks in with an armful of laundry
He loosens his bundle of stories

Like a reel of silk coming off from cocoon.
With open ears, my eyes follow his expressions
Yeah, Yeah, pretending to understand
I tactfully mimic holding the stomach
Following suit his burst of laughter
I am crying inwardly by my comical position
While he is joyous, engulfed in his own stories.

like a briefly passing shower
That won't even dampen an inch of hard soil
Finding their jokes utterly impossible to figure out
This late immigrant's common sense grows in
The language delivered in awkward gestures

Like a bouncing spring,
Bursting up from the boiling heat of a blasting furnace,
A golden dandelion
Roots on an inch of barren earth
With the persistence and the gentle leaf.
When reciting a stanza from a poem
Written in the mother tongue
That rose like the silken fog of the Eastern sky
Oh! the mellifluous quiver runs through me.

봄비 한 줌

얼마나 좋으면 삐죽삐죽
벌어진 주둥이 다물지 못하는 조것들 좀 봐
부풀은 땅속의
애벌레들이여!
새싹들이여!
아무리 몸 달아도 아직은 빈
나뭇가지에 바싹 몸 붙이고 주둥이 맞대고 앉아
속살거리며, 속닥거리며
날개야 젖어라!
젖어도 좋아 봄비인걸 뭐
어머나! 간지럽게
조것들 하는 짓 좀 봐

A Handful of Spring Rain

Look at them ——

Unable to close their beaks in utter happiness

To all the grubs within the swollen earth!

To all the new leaves!

Heeding impatience,

The birds whisper and chatter

Beak–to–beak

With their bodies leaning coles to still empty

brancher.

Wings, dampen!

It's all right; it's only the spring rain

Ah, what a sight! Look upon them and be tickled

by their cute gestures

이웃의 향기

이천우

오랜 이웃
세월의 이끼처럼 애틋한 정이 배어
흉허물 없이 속사정 펼치는
얽히고 설킨 나무 뿌리 같은 친구가 몇 있다.

집안 되어 대소사(大小事) 함께 나누는 남자
수밀도(水蜜桃) 같은 달콤한 여자
언제나 그 환한 웃음에
이 세상이 환해진다

아주 잘 익은 술에 취하여
세상 이야기 하다 보면 이 세상은 정말 향기롭다

정든 이웃들아
짙게 묻은 향기가
어느 꽃보다 곱구나.

Neighbor's Fragrance

Chun U Lee

Translated by Yearn Hong Choi

I have several good neighbors
Who are connected
As if they are redwood trees
Sharing their roots.

Men share football and baseball games.
Women share the cooking in the kitchen:
They make the world happy.

The world is beautiful when we talk about our
children
Over good wine,
And when we are intoxicated.

My neighbors are prettier than the flowers
In our garden.

기우제

잔디가 황달 걸려 누워 있다

비는 달포를 오지 않는데
소나기 한 차례 오간다고
멍청한 예보를 한다
앞을 아는 예보는 예보가 아니다
열파 주의보는 노인의 진액을 말리고
삣적 마른 토끼 한 놈이
시들거리는 야채 밭을 기웃기웃 댄다
천근 햇볕에 눌린 내 마음도
한 줄기 소나기가 아쉬운데
왕이라도 나와서 기우제를 지내야지

누군가 비를 만드는 사람이
천상(天上)에 살고 있었으면
좋으련만

Heat Wave

My lawn is no longer green;
and is becoming brown.

No rain in the last two months.
No afternoon shower in the forecast again.
A desert is coming.
Who knows?
A skinny rabbit is trying to steal
carrots in my backyard.
The Earth needs rain.

The King should come out to the altar
To pray for rain.
Is there a rainmaker in heaven?

포토맥 강가에 서서

이택제

불 뿜던 포연 가마득히 삼키우고
강가의 단풍나무 핏빛 어린 여울목
치열했던 전화(戰火) 그림자만 남아
소곤대며 설레는 포토맥 강물결

천 년을 회귀하는 푸른 저 하늘
솔개 떼 높이 날고
흰 물새 은빛 두 날개 펼쳐
한 폭 그림일레

남과 북, 뿌리 얽힌 역사의 아픈 자리
수백 년 세월 안고 그 넋을 되새기며
오색꽃 숲 둘러피는 하퍼스 페리 언덕

남북의 피 짙은 함성
골 깊은 정적 가르며
기적소리 메아리치는 철길따라
어망 엮듯 얼싸안은 다리밑

진혼지 전령의 후예인가
비둘기만 그 날의 시린 상흔
햇살 입고 조아린다

검은 핏줄 인권 외치며
봉기했던 존 브라운
포승줄에 묶여 가던 낡은 소방서앞
노예해방 목놓아 부르던 남과 북의 격전지

자유의 꿈 일깨우고
꽃 지듯 산화한 팻말만이 외로워서
고함소리 그 의미 묻어 두고
사라진 목숨의 움
함성의 둑은 터져
손잡고 얼싸안은 역사의 강변
그 자취 스러진 강가
쑥부쟁이 꽃은 희고
민들레 꽃씨 하얀 달무리로 둘렀다

티눈같이 돋아나는 역사의 뒤안길
피비린내 씻어버린 암벽의 층계 밟고
굽이로 끝없는 꽃숲의 철길 따라
고향에 오듯 옛자취 찾아드는 인파의 물결

화합과 평화안고
하염없이 흐르는 포토맥강 푸른 물결
거대한 아메리카 수도 워싱턴을 적시우고
오십 성좌 반짝이는 성조기의 깃발 아래
풀벌레 소리 쏟아지는 강여울
눈썹 같은 낮달 안고
역사의 강물은 흐른다

At the Harpers Ferry

Taek Jae Lee

Translated by Myong Hee Kim

An old beam stood there silently
In the midst of crimson autumn leaves
Like a long shadow of the fierce battle
The river whispered in its ripples

In the timeless blue skies
A hawk soared high and
The white wings of seagulls
Floated like silvery glide
The place of painful history
The crossing point of the North and

The South in bloody conflicts
On the mountain hills of the Harpers Ferry
Wild flowers were beautifully blooming
As if to remember the perished souls

The place John Brown fought
For the right of the black people
The Engine House where
John Brown was arrested

Out of the back alleys of history
Tourists came in groups
Stepping on the blood stained stone stairs
Like homecoming travelers seeking
The traces of forgotten memories

The blue water of Potomac River
Flows in peace and harmony
Through the capital city of the Great America
Under the Stars and Strips of the America Flag

The historic river water flows
Along the bird chirping river banks
Embracing a white moon in her bosom

후레지아꽃

친구가 안겨 준
한 묶음 후레지아꽃 속의
노란 리본이 속살거렸다
한 줄기의 꽃 향기를
그대에게 남겨두고 부르는
나의 노래는 어떠한 의미겠냐고……

사운대는 꽃샘바람
봄이 제 떠난
친구의 손목잡고 미사가던 좁은 사잇길
붐비는 사람 헤치며 지나친
뒷골목 작은 꽃집 앞
망울져 피어나던 후레지아의 노란 꽃향
친구가 보듬고 간
성모동산 장미 꽃밭에 뿌려 놓았다

흰구름 노 저어가는 푸른 하늘에
친구가 띄어 놓은 작은 기도
돌아오지 않는 세월의 강을 건너
오직 부활의 날 불려질 그 노래

Freesia Flowers

Translated by Sue LaPlant

A bundle of freesia
A gift from a friend
The tied yellow ribbon whispers in my ear
Whether I knew the meaning of a song
delivered to you
by the fragrance of a flower

Spring together with a chill breeze
Walked hand in hand of the narrow path
Making a way through the crowds
In front of a small florist in the back alley
Clusters of yellow at their peak fragrance
Armful of freesia in memory of a friend
I scattered around the rose garden she loved
Where a statue of Mother Mary stood

A humble prayer from my friend
to the flowing clouds in the blue sky
Cross the one—way river of the time passages
A song will resonate only on
the day of resurrection

3부

자식

이혜란

칡 두렁
혼을 묶던 날
능금색 볼의 파란 새순
신의 숨결 듣는다

작은 날개짓
뿌리 끝에 사랑 부으면
잔잔한 감동
기다림은 습관 되어

아이의 목소리는
고장 난 레코드처럼
돌아가고……

용암에 녹는 애간장
끊이지 않는 그리움
세월이 돌아서도
잊지 못하는 사람

모진 세월
문득 눈에 띈 이방인
사랑 접는 연습은
눈시울 삼키는 고행

A Child

Hea Lan Lee

Translated by Sue LaPlant

On one blissful day
Born is a child with gathered up soul
I listen with amazement
to God's breath in a new life
of apple-colored cheeks

When deepest love is poured onto a child
His new exploration each day
carves an impression in my heart
Waiting has become a painful pattern

Sound of the child's chatter
plays in my mind over and over
as if a broken record

Unbearable heartache as if melting in lava
Endless yearning
Although time passes on
he forever remains in my heart

Under the foothill of the time passage
I see a stranger at my door
Oh, letting the love fly away
is a heart−wrenching exercise

노파

숨이 턱에 차 오른 중천
사르르 보듬는 햇살
빗장 풀고
대문 활짝 열어 두면
인기척 소리
성인되어 떠난 어린 발자국 소리

모진 생
허리에 붙어
부서지는 아픔
푸르름 잃은 나무
할미꽃 같은 자태

벌들이 떠난 빈 벌집처럼
아직도 들리는 벌떼 소리
오늘은 멀리간 아들
소식 전해 오려나
양지 바른 곳 졸고 있는 어머니……

토담집에
온기 불어 넣고

바람에 헛기침 묻어 내면
부대끼며 사는 소리
그리워

An Old Woman

The Sun hung in the midst of sky
emits soft—hued sunlight down to earth
After unlocking the wooden—gate
And leaving the front door wide open
She hears the sound of someone
Perhaps, footsteps of the adult son returning home

Time flew, where did it go?
Passage of time heavily stamped on her back
pain lingers as if it's about to break
Same fate as a tree of late autumn
A hunch backed woman just like a wilting flower

Even at a deserted beehive
buzzing sound of bees still linger on
Today she might hear news
from a son who left for a faraway place
Mother falls asleep in a sunny spot

Warm up the house
built of clay and stone
Let out a dry cough to the wind
longing for the sound of hustling
of the bygone days

강가에서

임창현

겨울 강가에 앉아 있다
바람이 강물 위로 지나간다
어제가 흘러가고 오늘이 온다
또 내일이 잇따른다.
강물에 해 하나 잠겨 있다
바람은 시간이 우는 소리,
시간이 죽는 소리,
바람이 강물 속 해 흔들고 지나간다
하늘이 고향인 바람은
아무데서고 불어온다
회색머리 쥔 바람 하늘로 흩날릴 때
내 노을도 가까이 배오지만
강 위 내려놓으면
슬퍼하지 말아라 강은 말하며 간다
아무리 보아도 바람은 물보다 더 투명해서
둘이는 보이지 않게 섞이고
강은 바람 손잡고 함께 간다
하늘 해 구름도 들어온 강

물길 타면 나도 바람 되고 강물 된다

바람은 강에서처럼 내 작은 가슴에

한 줄기 강 심어 놓고 온몸 돌다가

뼈에서 일어나 다시 강으로 간다

강에는 꼭 바람이 있다

나도 강 따라 바람 되어 간다

강 되어 간다

슬퍼하지 마라 말하는

강물 되어 간다.

At a Riverbank

Chang Hyun Yim

Translated by Sue LaPlant

Sitting at a winter riverbank

I watch the winds flirting with the water

Gone is yesterday, today has arrived

Tomorrow, too, shall follow

The sun is drowned in the water

Weeping sound of time comes as winds

Agonizing over time lost, time dying?

Winds stir up the sun in the water and flee away

Winds can come from every direction

For the sky is their home
Winds rush off to the sky
Scattering about my graying hair
Oh, must it be the signal of my parting day nearing
When I unload my heart on the water, the river
whispers
"Don't be sad!" as it flows away
Wind is clearer than water even up close
So the wind and water blend indistinguishably well
Hand in hand, they flow away together

The river now embraces the sky, sun, and clouds
Along the river, I am the wind, I am the river
Wind circulates in my body as it does over the
river
Then poof! It rises up from the bone and heads to
the river
River always summons winds
I, too, become wind following the river
I become the river
"Don't grieve!" as the river would say
I, too, console myself as I flow down

추억을 위한 프렐류드

추억은 팔지 못한다
마지막 남는 추억은 고향이다
고향은 팔지 않는다

추억은 씨다
눈 감고도 만날 수 있는 희망의 씨앗들
모두 모여 살고 있는 기억의 방

우리를 지탱하고 있는 것은
내일이 아니다
어제이다 어제의 뿌리다
어제가 잡고 있는 뿌리

언제나 어제였다
그 어제 속에 있는 내일
추억 속 미래

추억은 희망이다
저 앞에 보이는 과거

A Prelude to Memory

Memory cannot be bought
The last memory deeply embedded in our hearts
is our hometown
Hometown does not sell out

Memory is a seed
Seeds of hope, visible seeds even with eyes closed
A memory of the room, crammed but happy,
as the whole family living together

What supports us
is not tomorrow
but yesterday, the roots of yesterday
Roots deeply held by yesterday

It is always yesterday
Tomorrow will be born from yesterday
Future exists within memory

Memory is our hope
Bygone days stand right in front of us

한 사내

장혜정

강가에 앉아
한 사내가 웁니다
아카시아 이파리 손에 들고

언제부터인지 강 건너 저쪽에
두 눈을 붙박은 채
오지 않는 나룻배 기다립니다

기다리다 지치면
아카시아 한 잎씩 따서
강물에 띄웁니다

그때마다 강물이 가만히 다가와
그 서러움 한 잎씩
업고 갑니다

어느 새 어둑어둑 날 저물자
오늘도 빈 수레 하나

그리움만 가득 싣고
그 사내 뒤를 꺼어~꺽 울며 따라갑니다

A Man

Hae Jung Chang
Translated by Yearn Hong Choi

One man is crying
at the edge of the river,
holding an acacia leaf in his hand

He has been waiting for a ferry boat
coming from the other side of the river.
his two eyes have been fixed at the boat in
mirage.

He has been taking one leaf from the acacia tree
after another, and placing it on the river
patiently all day.

The river takes his sorrow
one by one,
whenever he places the green leaf onto the river.
 The night is falling:

one empty carriage full of yearning
is following the man's hoarse crying.

참전용사

메모리얼 데이 행사 초대석에
부동 자세로 앉아 있는
앳된 이라크 참전 병사 하나

폭탄 맞아 일그러진 코와
부기가 덜 빠진 푸른 눈동자
채 아물지 않은 피 멍든 입술

사람들은
의아한 듯
반은 연민의 얼굴로
보는 듯 안 보는 듯
힐끔거리며 스쳐 지나가고

귀밑머리 파르스름한
열아홉 살 병사의 마음은
아랑곳없이 대서양 건너 지중해로
달려가 피비린내나는 전장을 뒤지며
오직 전우들의 안녕을 살피고 싶을 뿐

풍악 소리가 낯선

어린 병사의 목덜미를 감싸 안고
살아 돌아와 고맙다고 어루만져 주는
오월의 훈풍

A war veteran

One young soldier
wounded in the Iraq War
sat on a chair straight
at the Memorial Day ceremony.

His broken nose,
his swollen and blue eyes, and
his bloody lips
were not all pretty

The men and women attending the ceremony
surprised at his presence, or shocked.
they were all uncomfortable.

The 19−year old soldier
must be concerned about his fellow soldiers
who stationed in the war field
across the Atlantic and Mediterranean Sea

The breeze in May
was just comforting the young soldier
at the ceremony.

길을 만드는 것

전현자

나는 때때로
방향감각을 잃고 길 위에 서 있을 때가 있다
내 안의 길들이
하나둘씩 유실되어 가는 걸 볼 때
더 이상
누구들의 절실한 우선순위가 아님을 느낄 때
가까운 사람들에게서조차
내 목소리가 자주 지워짐을 당할 때
여백의 허한 시간 위에서
찻잔처럼 마주할 친구 하나 얻지 못할 때
삶의 무거운 순간들을
철저히 혼자 버텨야 할 때……
그럴 때마다
길을 잃고 망연히 서 있을 때가 있다.

사랑받지 못하는 것은 길을 잃게 하는 것이다.

그 횟수가 늘어갈수록

"

기대했던 주변을 향해
원망의 촉수를 높이고
가슴에 빗금 치는 일도 늘어
길은 점점 더 갇히고
빛마저 아슴아슴 잠긴다.

사랑하지 않는 것은 길을 잃는 것이다.

그러나
원망의 촉수를 안으로 거두고
조용히 마음을 꿇으면
어둠으로부터 다시 밝아오는
관용과 용서의 지우개가 있어
허다한 빗금들이 다 지워지고
길은 사방으로 열린다.

사랑하는 것은 길을 만드는 것이다.

To Create a Road

Hyun Ja Jun

Translated by Sue LaPlant

I occasionally get lost,

And stand at a crossroad, uncertain of the direction

When I watch the roads within me

Disappear one by one

When a realization occurs

I no longer am people's priority

When my voice carries no weight,

even with people close and dear to me

When I am unable to find a friend

To share a leisurely cup of tea

When I must endure the heavy burden of life all alone

These are the times

I feel lost

and unable to find my direction

Not being loved makes one lose a road

The more one expects from others

The more disappointments grow

The wounds carved in our hearts pierce deeper
and wider

The roads close one by one
and even the lights get dimmer little by little

Not to love is a way to lose a road.

Nevertheless

When we put the blames on ourselves

And silently repent

Light can shine again onto the darkness

Generosity and forgiveness are restored

Numerous wounds are healed

And the roads are open to all directions.

Loving others is the way to create a road.

씨

까만 점 하나로 화려한 대물림
난, 네 정체를 그냥 '씨' 라고만 부른다.
이름도 조상도 너만 보아선 가늠 못한다.
겨우내 흙 속에 묻혀 무엇을 하는지도 수수께끼다.
다만,
봄이 되면 언 땅도 뚫어내는 가상한 힘이 있다는 것만 알
뿐이다.
내민 얼굴을 보고서야 아하! 그거였구나 안다.

바늘 하나 찌를 공간 없는 그 방 어디에
잎, 꽃, 열매, 향기, 색깔
맥박 뛰어 피 도는 흔적도 없는데
부활의 생명까지……
입김 하나로 우주를 굴리는
창조주의 기운이 아니고서야
그러기엔
암만해도 네 방이 너무 좁다.

Seed

Glorious beginning of next generation from a
small black dot
Your identity, I just call it 'seed'.
I can neither tell your name nor recognize your
ancestors.
It is a mystery what you do under earth the entire
winter.
I only know
You have a great power to penetrate frozen earth
in spring.
When you poked through the ground and show
your face,
It makes me realize, "A−ha, it's you!"

Such a tiny being, not even a needle can pierce
through you
Not a leaf, flower, fruit, fragrance, or color exists
Neither trace of heart beat, nor a circulation of
blood
And yet the power of resurrection⋯⋯
It must be God who can turn the earth with
One puff of breath
Otherwise, your stature is just too miniscule.

쉐난도아의 가을

정애경

창을 열면
후끈, 달아오른 뙤약볕
옥수수 알 꿈들이
줄지어 영글어 간다

한 여름 비바람에 적시어진
푸른 옷 벗어 말리며
찬 바람 숨결 타고
여름이
떠날 채비를 한다

구월의 끄트머리마저도
놓쳐버린
마른 햇살 쏟아지는 날
그을린 바람 타고
누워 있는 변두리
쉐난도아
갈빛, 어느 새 내려와
누우런 병풍 펼쳐 놓는다

Autumn in Shenandoah

Ae Kyung Chung
Translated by Sue LaPlant

As I open a window
Suddenly blazing sunshine rushes in
Dreams are ripening all lined up
just like corn kernels

Drenched in summer shower
Green leaves spread high for drying
On the wings of the cool breezes are flowing about
Summer
Is preparing to leave

September slipped away
Leaving dry sunlight to pour out
Under the sunbathed winds
Lies the hills of the outskirts
Shenandoah
Sudden appearance of autumn color
Stretches out like a golden—yellow screen

어머니

나에겐
온몸에 흐르는
유산이 있습니다

어릴 적
눈망울이 커지며 사색에 잠기던 날
부지런한 개미를 바라보며
깨달았지요

온몸, 온몸 열어 뜨거운
핏덩이로 쏟아 낸 순간부터
어머니는 날 위해
기도하셨는가 봅니다

하늘이
눈발을 퍼붓고 빗살을 후려쳐도
세상이
실망을 가져오고 슬픔을 가져와도
그래도
절망을 꿈꾸지 않는 것은
불타는

내리사랑 때문인가 봅니다

구름이 햇빛을 가려도
온몸에 햇살을 느끼게 하는 것은
으뜸으로 빛나는
어머니의
사랑과 채찍질
때문이지요

Mother

I am blessed with
An invaluable inheritance
That flows through my entire body

One day in youth
While pondering upon an eye-popping thought
It came to a realization by watching
the swarms of busily working ants

From the moment she embraced
A blood covered newborn
My mother must have prayed
For me

Though the sky pours down on me,
Rainstorms and blizzards
Though the world brought upon me
Disappointments and sorrows
Still
I wouldn't dare to dream of despair
All due to my mother's ever present and tireless
love

Even when the clouds hide the sun
My whole body feels the penetrating warmth of the
sun
It's all because of the greatest power of
My mother's eternal love
And encouragement

집 할부금

정영희

한 달을 하루같이
집 할부금 낼 버거움 안은 채
그래도 꾸려가게 하는 힘

한 해를 넘나들며
세월의 무심만 탓하지 말라
타이르는 경고장

한 세기를 나누며
삶의 새로운 생기를 불어넣는
꿈의 집

삶이 산 재산 되어
후회 없는 내일을 기약하는
약속의 땅
거기에 모두 있었네

Mortgage Payments

Yung Whi Chung

Translated by Eunhwa Choe

A month seems like a day,
The burden to make mortgage payments,
But with the strength of persevering

As I am passing over the years,
Do not blame the passing time
The warning letter dictates,

Sharing a century,
A dream house,
Provides a new energy of life.

The life itself becomes richer,
Promising tomorrow of no regrets,
The land of promise ——

Everything was there.

가을 산

젊음이 장작불처럼
가슴을 불태울 땐
까맣게 숯이 된 줄 알았는데
불씨 하나
그래도
살아 있었나봐

뉘엿이 지는 저녁 해는
하늘을 불태우고
빨갛게 물든 노을 속
산 그림자 하나 외로움에
떨고 서 있네

오고야 말 시간을 위해
남은 불씨 하나 당겨
가을 산 붉게 물들이고
낙엽들 머지않아 대지 위를 떠돌면
당신은
눈감고 호수 속에 갇혀
더 붉게 붉게 타오르리라
그림자마저 떠나보내고
칡흙 같은 어둠 속에 혼자 서서

Autumn Mountain

When youthfulness stoked
The fire with in the heart
I thought it became charcoal
But a small flint
Must have
Lived on

The evening sun about to set
Flames up the sky
In the crimson tinted sky
A mountain shadow
Trembles in loneliness

For the inevitable time
Ignites the remaining flint
Tinting the autumn mountain in red
You will
Close your eyes and be locked in the lake
Will burn redder and redder
After sending the shadows away
Standing alone in the total darkness

밤

조형주

깊은 밤
누군가 부르는 소리 있어
창 열고 일어서면
창밖 바람찬 먼 하늘
별들만 소곤대고 있었다
없는 것으로 가슴 가득
채워져 오는 하늘

은하수,
유성은
누구의 눈물일까
지구가 잠자는 밤에는
별들도 나처럼 깨어 있구나

그리움은 별이 되고 달무리 되고
부르면, 말하면, 들릴 것 같아
가슴으로 소리쳐도
메아리는 이슬 같은 별빛

밤하늘은 그렇게 빈 것이었다
가득한 것이었다

Night

Hyung Joo Cho

Translated by Sue LaPlant

In the deepest night
Someone called for me
Stirring from deep slumber, I look out the window
I see only the stars whispering amongst themselves
in the windy sky far away
The sky fills my heart
with nothing but emptiness

A Milky Way
and the falling stars
whose tears are they
When the earth sleeps
stars stay awake just as I am
Longing has become the stars and the halo
Should I call, I think they can hear,
I shout for them from my heart
Only the echoes shine in the starlight

A night sky is empty,
filled only with emptiness

만남

작은 가슴으로는
모두 다 품을 수 없어
차라리
바다로 가는
냇물이고 싶다

감추어 온 긴 세월
아픈 내 옹이
드러내어 이제는
전하고 싶다

서로를 잃었던 깊은 숲
사슴이었던 너에게는
호수이고 싶다

기다림은
언제나 고통이지만
나무 되어
낙엽이 되어
침묵으로 그렇게 기다리고 싶다
꿈꾸고 싶다

바다로 가는
강물이고 싶다

Meeting

I' d rather be a stream
that flows to the ocean
for I cannot hold them all
within my small bosom

Though I have hidden my deep wounds
for a long, long time
Now I wish to reveal the scars
and speak of them

In the thickets of forest where we lost ourselves
You were an innocent deer
I now wish to be a lake for you

Although waiting is
always a torture
I will become a tree
and remain as autumn leaves
I will wait silently for a long time
I wish to dream so

I wish to be a river

that flows to the ocean

호수

최은숙

호수는 강물처럼 흐르지 않습니다
늘 그 자리에 머물러
당신의 잔잔한 이야기를 듣고 있을 뿐입니다

호수는 파도처럼 소리내어 울지 않습니다
당신의 눈물이 고여
고요히 가라앉기만을 바랄 뿐입니다

호수는 누군가 던지는 돌을 피하지 않습니다
그 돌을 가라앉히어
가장 낮은 곳에 품어안을 뿐입니다

호수는 거울보다 더 맑은 거울입니다
가만 바라보고 있으면
마음 깊은 곳까지 고루 비추어내니 말입니다

A Lake

Eun Sook Choi

Translated by Sue LaPlant

A lake does not flow away, unlike a river
It remains eternally in the same place
and just listens to your secret tales

A lake does not wail, unlike ocean waves
when welled up with tears
it only waits hoping it would settle calmly

A lake does not avoid pebbles thrown at it
Rather, it would cherish them
By embracing them in the depth of its bosom

A lake is clearer than a mirror
when it is gazed at
it reveals even the deepest part of its heart

옷

사람이 입는
옷
옷

사람 닮은
한글 이름
옷

세상에서
가장 아름답고
옷다운 글자
옷

Clothes

Humans dress themselves in
Clothes
Similar in appearance as human
Korean script
Clothes
And the most appropriately formed script
In the world
Clothes

새벽기도 가는 길

최임혁

스란치마 잘잘 끌며 봄바람 걸어오니
연초록 나뭇가지 샛별 따라 길 나선다
개나리 팡팡 터지는 소리 새벽종이 놀란다

A Road to an Early Morning Prayer

Im Hyok Choe
Translated by Sue LaPlant

As spring winds come hurriedly
blowing women's long skirts
Light−green leaves sprout out
following the morning stars
Loud sound of forsythia blossoms popping out
startles the morning bell

봄밤

청아한 피리 소리
달빛 타고 흐르니

포럼한 매화꽃이
잠깨어 춤을 추고

여울물 나직한 속삭임은
긴긴 밤을 엮는다.

Spring Night

The elegant sound of a flute
Flows through the moonlight

Iridescent plum blossoms
Woke up to dance

Soft whispers of a shallow brook
Lulls this sleepless long night

사랑의 노래 1

최현규

그대여
숲 속 깊은 오솔길을 따라
나무와 꽃, 들풀을 헤치고 오라

일출과 노을의 동화 속에 꿈을 찾으라

맑은 공기 작은 샘
생수가 흐르는 곳
나는 고요한 숲속의 빈터

쉼 찾는 그대여
오라
나
그대의 빈 의자가 되리

A Love Song 1

Hyun Kyu Choi

Translated by Yearn Hong Choi

Darling,
Come to me
Pass through the trees, flowers and wild grasses
Along the trail in the woods.

Discover my dream
From the sunrise to the sunset
And read fairy tales in between.

Fresh air, spring water, and stream
Surround and fill an empty quiet spot
Deep inside the woods.

Darling
Looking for peaceful rest,
Come to me.
I will be a chair for you
In the woods.

사랑의 노래 2

밤하늘
까만 화선지에 흩뿌려 있는
하얀 별 꽃 가루

외로운 그믐달 곁
한 송이 별을 따
그대 가슴에 포근히 안겨주리

그저, 말없이
하늘 도화지에 별 빛 모아 엮어
그리운 내 마음 실어 보내리

바다 건너에서
기도하는
내 사랑 그대에게

A Love Song 2

White flower petals
Scattered on the dark rice paper
In the night sky.

I will pick up the most beautiful flower petals
Beside the lonely crescent moon and
Make them a bouquet
And give it to you.

I will send you my love
Without any word,
But just with the flowers made from the star light
In our night sky.

I love you passionately
Praying for my health, safety and success
From the other side of the Ocean.

칠순

허 권

칠십이 되어 가던 날
무척 당황해야 했다

속을 들여다보니, 마치 우물처럼
그 분은 보이지 않고
온갖 것 먼지만 쌓여 있다

아직 십년 더, 성경대로라면
지금부터라도 무엇을 해야 하나
그냥 웃으며 살아갈까?
아니면
누군가 날 위해 기도하던 사람
찾아 나설까?
아니면
시간 없어도 그 그 분

Approaching 70

Kwon Hu

Translated by Sue LaPlant

Approaching 70
I was quite perplexed

When I looked into my heart, as if it was a well
I could not find him
But only the accumulated dust

Still ten more years, citing the Bible
What should I do starting now
Just pass the time leisurely
Or
Begin on a journey to find people
Who prayed for me?
Or
Although not much time left, for Him

엽서

빛 바랜
책 갈피 속에 곱게 접어둔
그리운 엽서 꺼내
오늘은 눈물로 그림을 그리자

저 산 너머 어둔 하늘
슬픈 달은 지우자
아직도 어쩌지 못하는 이 마음은
무슨 색깔로 칠할까

그리고 네가 좋아하던
자목련 한 그루도 심어야지
그대에게 가는 길
다시 이십 년이 걸린다 해도
너와 목련 꽃 그늘 아래서 만날 수 있는
그 날을 그리자

A Post Card

A precious post card faded with age
Safeguarded between the leaves of a book
Today, I will draw a picture on it
With Tears

Over the mountain in the dark sky
The sad moon, I shall erase
The unstoppable longing of my heart
What color should it be

A purple magnolia you loved,
I shall plant it
The road to your heart
Even if it takes another 20 years
I will draw our meeting day
Under the magnolia blossoms